MY FIRST BEST FRIEND

NEVER LOOSE HOPE

G.SAINATH ROHIT

Copyright © G.sainath Rohit
All Rights Reserved.

<u>My First Best Friend</u>

My First day of the school, I got new friends , new environment, new faces and I was afraid. I was siting in the last bench of middle row. My First class teacher name was vijay Lakshmi Teacher. Class started, all the students were getting Introduced. Then, I heard his name, "Abhiroop".

I just wondered what type of name it is !!?. His name was different from others.

I taught that "Abhiroop" meaning is that, he will change his roop (shape) depending on the behaviour of the students. haha i used to think like that.

But i was wrong, day by day he was good to others and me too...don't know why ,he look special for me.

One day we sat together and he was normal with me. I don't know what to talk. I said to myself that...(arey yaar he is not a girl)

Slowly slowly we became close and we started knowing about each other very well.

I was being true with him and he too was being the same with me.

I was happy that i got a friend who could bare all my happiness and sadness.

I requested god that, not to break our friendship.

Since first class he was my best friend. We will sit together, eat together, go together play together and many more.

I was happy with my friendship and suddenly one atom bomb was blast in our 3rd class.

Sameera, she was very cute and very sweet. Obviously Children will be loyal and sweet to their friends. All the class hate her because she will be not close to anyone. She want to sit alone and study. She was family wali bachhi !

having crush in schood days was Awesome feeling in the life. and that too in 3rd class...LOL. !

I was having a crush on her. I said to abhiroop that i like her.

On the cultural event day we all became friends. All were dancing and playing together. There was a big smile on our face, all were meeting eachother and making friends . we all were happy at that moment.

In the next day, all are present expect sameera. i was dissapointed that she is absent but unfortunately she came to school. she was late.

Finally she sat behind me.

Abhiroop sat beside me, obviously best friends will have so much stuff to talk and we will make fun of each other and laugh like an idiots.

If we get scoldings from our teacher or sir , automatically smile comes to our face.

We can't control it. And the day has come, finally sameera sawed me and talked to me regarding subject related doubt . I was managing that i know everything. But My idiot abhiroop was laughing. And she also started laughing at me.

I was like shit-yaar.

I scolded him a lot after the school. He was like, ok i will make you both move closer. I was like, ok done.

And next day she started sitting behind us....as usually we will do jokes, and slowly she turned back and started laughing.

From that day i and abhiroop and cracking jokes in every period.

In class, if i was punished, abhi will crack jokes on me and i will laugh on him in front of all.

If he was punished, i will crack a joke on him in front of all and my main focus will be on sameera that, she is enjoying my jokes or else she is feeling annoying.

I got to know from her smile that she was enjoying my jokes.

I was happy with my bestfriend Abhiroop and my favourite person sameera.

Day by day she was becoming close to me and my jokes. She said, she is happy to have me and abhiroop in her life.

We 3 became good friend in 3rd class.

One fine day in front of all she clenched my chicks and said you are soo cute and chubby chubby. I was shocked! I was blushing by lying on the bench.

And the same she said to abhiroop. and she also said that, she likes him.

I was like hoo....ok.......my mind was blank .i didn't understand anything. She was looking at abhiroop and smiling and he was doing showoff in front of her by saying, hoo....Really !?.

I suddenly stood up and i said i will come in few minutes.

I went to restroom, and my tears are unstoppable. I was blank.

I thought, if she like abhiroop it's not his fault. I have to change my mindset and be positive on them.

On that day i was not cracking jokes on abhiroop and i was not close to sameera also. Sameera have been trying to talk to me everyday. But i was just avoiding her like nibba nibbi love story.

Abhiroop got to know the reason behind my silence .He was not sorry to me.I was like it's ok .

Suddenly we got barriers in between us for few days. I was ok with sameera and abhiroop. I said to them i don't have any bad intention on you both.

They were clear that, they are not in love. But im not that type of person which, i can't handle the vibe and closeness between them. They were ok with me. But i was not ok with them. I can't see my best friend loving my crush.

But in the matter of friendship, I was ready to sacrifice her, And I did. But unfortunately she took TC in 4th class and she took admission in another school. Abhiroop was in a shock by listening that she is no more in our school. And I was totally broken. I cried a lot for her.

But we didn't tried to get her address, contact number and her school name nothing we knew about her. We are not CID officers to investigate about her and drag the details..! Come on yaar we are in 4th class only. We don't even got the thought to take her number. But that was a Good feelings in my school life.

I don't know where is sameera, how she is and what she is doing.

I just knew that her name is sameera, she has curly hairs and she is cute and sweet. Still now i remember her face. If i ask the same question to abhiroop in 2019. he was like, who is she??.

So coming to 4th class. Our class teacher was Usha rani teacher. We were growing up day by day. I have learned new badwords from abhiroop and i was applying to my all friends. I was very happy to apply them the badwords. I was enjoying by scolding others.At one day i and abhi were sitting at last bench.

We was having hind period. We were soo naughty in the class. We are cracking many jokes and laughing like a hell.We have an habit to lift up the bench from below with the foot.

We were lifting up and also we were scared of falling down,Our aim is to lift the bench up and we have to get tense of falling down and we have to Laugh. That's it !

We are in last bench and be have a gap between wall and last bench. We do not have a support to make balance at our back.

Finally it was my turn, i lifted the bench more than the limit and we have fallen down in slow motion. We hiding our faces with hands stick to the floor and our hindi madam came to us. She was like "Ayyooo are you ok beta"

She was pampering us and she was checking us that we are good or crying.But, we idiots were laughing non-stop.

We are in a hurry to cover our laughing face in front of our teacher.This was the memorable and unforgettable day in my life.

I still remember it and i laugh the same as i used to laugh before.After few days abhiroop said about his plan.

That, he was leaving with his family to his relatives house. Which is out of station. I started crying, i was begging him plz don't go. But he was helpless.

I was not in a good mood the whole day. I can't even imagine a day without him in the class. And i know i can't be far from him. His presence is oxygen for me.

But he was about to go next day. I made myself strong and i was like plz come soon. I will be waiting for you. He felt emotional about me. He too got tears. But he controlled.

All my friends were saying why are you crying like a girl, he will come back. Chill yaar....etc etc they were saying to me.

But i know what he is for me and what i feel about himr without his presence. He was the only best friend for me since 3 and 1/2 years. I can't even leave him like that.

Finally he went. From the day he went i was like "Nobitha waiting for his doraemon". Finally he was back after 1 week.

The day he came i gave him a tight hug and kiss on his chicks. All were like chiii chiiii. I was like hahahaha. Again my doors of Happiness were open by abhi, coming back to class.

Days passed on and one fine day i was not happy . This class was a hell to me all the Sections changed.Abhiroop is no more in my class.

I was in 'A' section and he was in 'B'. I just had a point in my mind that, sameera left, its ok i have abhiroop in my life, i was like no need to worry. I will be happy and make him happy this year too. But we got a long distance between us.

I got new friends, he also got new friends and i swear no one was like abhiroop . i was missing him from 2 to 3 weeks.

He was normal, no missing and nothing. We will meet only in lunch time and break time. That to only for few minutes. I was missing my true friend.

Now we are in 6th class again new friends and girls. Again distractions and masthi. I was doing all my masthi and enjoying all my days with new friends with Abhi.

I was feeling vere bad and he was also not willing to meet me as we used to meet before. Again we gather together in 9th class. He was still my best friend.

Again we sat together and all the fun and masthi repeat. And again girls, distraction etc. We have got more new friends in 9th class.

We were called as Junior 10th class. Again i got wounded with new friends, Rohit singh, sumit singh, ashish, Ashwin, Jai kumar, sai mahesh, saleem mallik, janghir mallik, Ruthvik kumar, dhanush, niharika.K , niharika.B, Deepika kothari, manav sharma, bhavya reddy goutam, pranay yadav, shanmukha, hrithik kumar, pavan kumar etc etc.

All colourful friends with colourful world. It was a new feeling to me. But i have never replaced Abhiroop among these. He is special for me and will be special for me throughout my life. We have done with our 10th class.

Somany feelings , emotions, and happiness we left behind. Ahiroop and all my friends left . I was soo depressed about leaving all . that's too all of sudden.

But it's life we have to move on. For every friendship day i used to go to abhiroop house and give him gifts. His mom n dad were so nice towards me and they too knew that i was his best-best-bestttt friend for his life.

But i was wrong about him. When i was in Degree i and my friend alpha went to abhiroop house to celebrate his birthday.

He came out with long hairs and thick Beard. He was looking handsome. I was very happy to see him after long time. I have contacted him so many times. But he was not in Hyderabad. He went out of station with his cousins.

And finaly met him on his birthday in my degree. He was studying b.tech and also he started his career in sports. I was so happy for him.

I and my Alpha made his birthday so special and awesome we were again laughing like out school days. That was the bond between me and abhiroop. alpha was alo my best friend, and he know everything about abhiroop.

we were laughing on the strees like mad people. one we bond together na we will not care anyone. we will have our own vibe of masthi and laundpana !

i have been never been lied to abhi and i have shared all my secrets to him......he is one of my loved person. you can know my value of friendship one you see both of us together.

After his birthday in 2019 we never met him again. In my life lots of things happened and i was very eagerly waiting to tell all my stuff to abhiroop.

I share with him everything including my personal life. But, after his birthday. I have contacted him 100 times 500 messages and went to his home many times. I have got to know that he got hired in photography job. He is very passionate about capturing images. he also have a camera tattoo on his right hand.

I got to knew it by his Instagram post.

I have seen all his posts on insta. all were amazing and it was like a pro Photographer. I have dropped a comment on his post and tried to DM him....then also no use. Now we are in 2022 till now im trying to contact him. I will go near his house and stand in front of his house .

I will stare at his door....i have a hope that he will definitely come outside. But that hope is still a dream for me. I have no guts to go to his house directly.

Because their is no response from the person since 3 years.Im still waiting for his reply and call. Because i don't want to miss a friend like Abhi.

May be, he may be busy......but im still waiting for his friendship to comeback and be as like we used to be before. I have to tell him many miracles which i have passed these many years .

Im not angry on him or i don't have any revenge on him. I just wanna make my friendship live. And with Ego and Attitude i don't want to loose his friendship. Because it's hard to find a friend like my ABHI.

Finally missing him a lot.....In life special people comes only once, once you miss them, they never gonna come back.!

Be in there presence when ever they are with you or in front of you. plz pause your ego and attitude in front of Loved once. they are the only person who likes you as how you are now !

they not gonna change your life, not gonna judge you, they not gonna show you attitude if they are true Friends.

See the life in prespective way, if Parents are our Road, Bridge is our friends, if traffice signal are our Exams, Traffice police are our Lecturers .

All will show us the Right way, but when and where to stop and where to escape is depend upon you. if you go through from all situation, you will get to know what are the difficulties you must face in future and it will be easy for you.

But, if you take shortcut from the galli (lane), you don't don't what is going to be the future and you will face many difficulties. think once !

Guys do you think I'm over reacting and being soo fool towards abhiroop. So many people said me that are yaar he is changed and he don't have the same special feeling towards you.

Just forget him just throw the fuck him away etc etc, they have said to me. But I never got bored and tired of his friendship. Because True Friendship is Hard to find.

Finally i waited a lot and i have moved from my native place hyderabad and shifted to Banglore. if i would be in Hyderabad i would have spoil my mind with uneven thoughts and undigested stuff thinking that why it happens only for me.

I was wrong ! It happens for everyone and maximum number of people can't handle it and they want to leave the situation and get rid of those people with whome they are suffering.

Im not suffering im just waiting for his reply and responce.

miss you my dear friend, in future i want to enjoy my
success with you if i fail i want to share my pain with
you......whatever the matter may be. But in my life you are
Mandatory !

STILL WAITING FOR YOUR REPLY...

Yours Lovingly Sainath Rohit.

Contents

www.ingramcontent.com/pod-product-compliance
Lightning Source LLC
Chambersburg PA
CBHW022048150726
47990CB00004B/1654